I AM A
TORNADO

DREW BECKMEYER

Atheneum Books for Young Readers
New York   London   Toronto   Sydney   New Delhi

ATHENEUM BOOKS FOR YOUNG READERS
An imprint of Simon & Schuster Children's Publishing Division
1230 Avenue of the Americas, New York, New York 10020
© 2023 by Drew Beckmeyer
Book design by Greg Stadnyk © 2023 by Simon & Schuster, Inc.
ATHENEUM BOOKS FOR YOUNG READERS is a registered trademark of Simon & Schuster, Inc.
Atheneum logo is a trademark of Simon & Schuster, Inc.
For information about special discounts for bulk purchases, please contact Simon & Schuster
Special Sales at 1-866-506-1949 or business@simonandschuster.com.
The Simon & Schuster Speakers Bureau can bring authors to your live event. For more information or to book an event,
contact the Simon & Schuster Speakers Bureau at 1-866-248-3049 or visit our website at www.simonspeakers.com.
The text for this book was set in Jost.
The illustrations for this book were rendered in cut paper.
Manufactured in China
0123 SCP
First Edition
2 4 6 8 10 9 7 5 3 1
Library of Congress Cataloging-in-Publication Data
Names: Beckmeyer, Drew, author.
Title: I am a tornado / Drew Beckmeyer.
Description: First edition. | New York : Atheneum Books for Young Readers, [2023] |
Audience: Ages 4 to 8. | Summary: An angry, destructive tornado picks up an empathetic cow, and when
Cow politely asks to be put down, the two enter a conversation that has some unforeseen results.
Identifiers: LCCN 2022005472 | ISBN 9781665916745 (hardcover) | ISBN 9781665916752 (ebook)
Subjects: CYAC: Tornadoes—Fiction. | Cows—Fiction. | Emotions—Fiction. | Conflict management—Fiction. | LCGFT: Picture Books.
Classification: LCC PZ7.1.B4349 Iah 2023 | DDC [E]—dc23
LC record available at https://lccn.loc.gov/2022005472

For Lee

I AM A TORNADO.

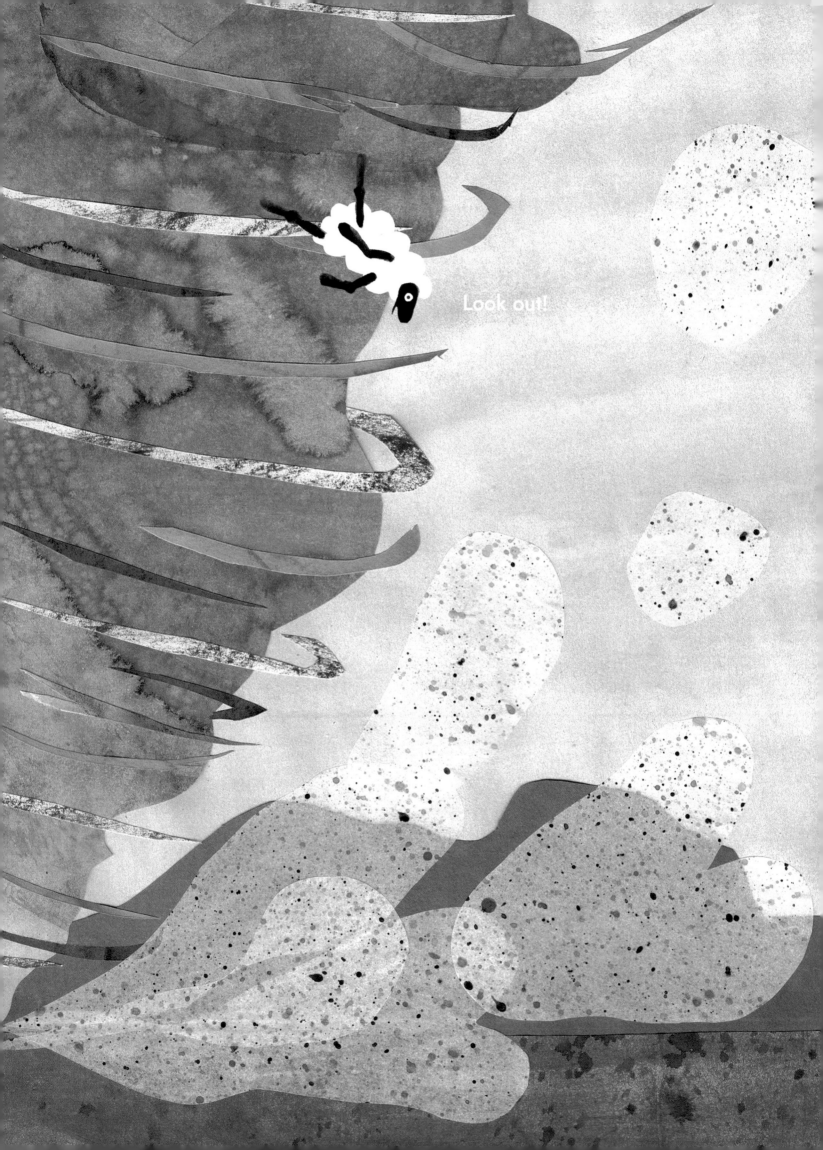

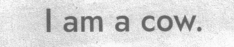

I am a cow.

I AM SO BIG
AND I AM SPINNING
SO FAST.

Argh.

Could you put me down?

NO.
WATCH THIS!

Hey,
someone could've
been in there.

I DON'T CARE.

Tornado,
is everything okay?

WHY WOULD I NOT BE
OKAY?

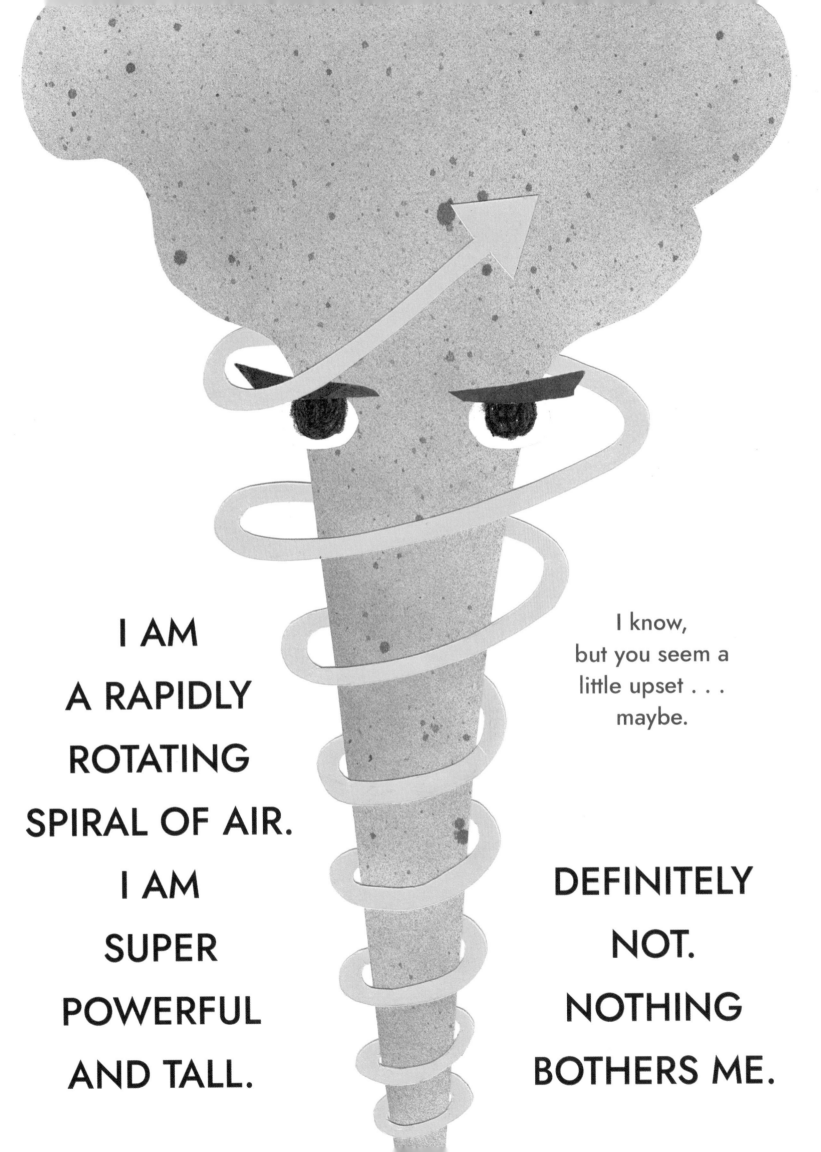

I AM
A RAPIDLY
ROTATING
SPIRAL OF AIR.
I AM
SUPER
POWERFUL
AND TALL.

I know,
but you seem a
little upset . . .
maybe.

DEFINITELY
NOT.
NOTHING
BOTHERS ME.

Nothing?

NOTHING.

Ever?

EVER.

WHAT WOULD
MAKE YOU THINK
I'M UPSET?

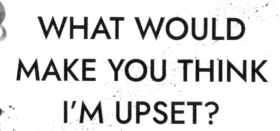

SO?

Well, you're
spinning
and yelling.

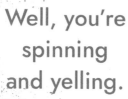

Okay, but . . .

WHY ARE THESE PEOPLE STARING AT ME?

Those scientists are probably
just curious about you.

I'M GONNA GO TOSS 'EM.

Wait.

Could you all
back up?
I think it just needs
some space
right now.

Oh, okay.
Sorry, Tornado.

With all these
violently changing cold winds
high in the sky,

and that warm air
rising from the ground,

I can see how it
would make anyone
a little irritable.

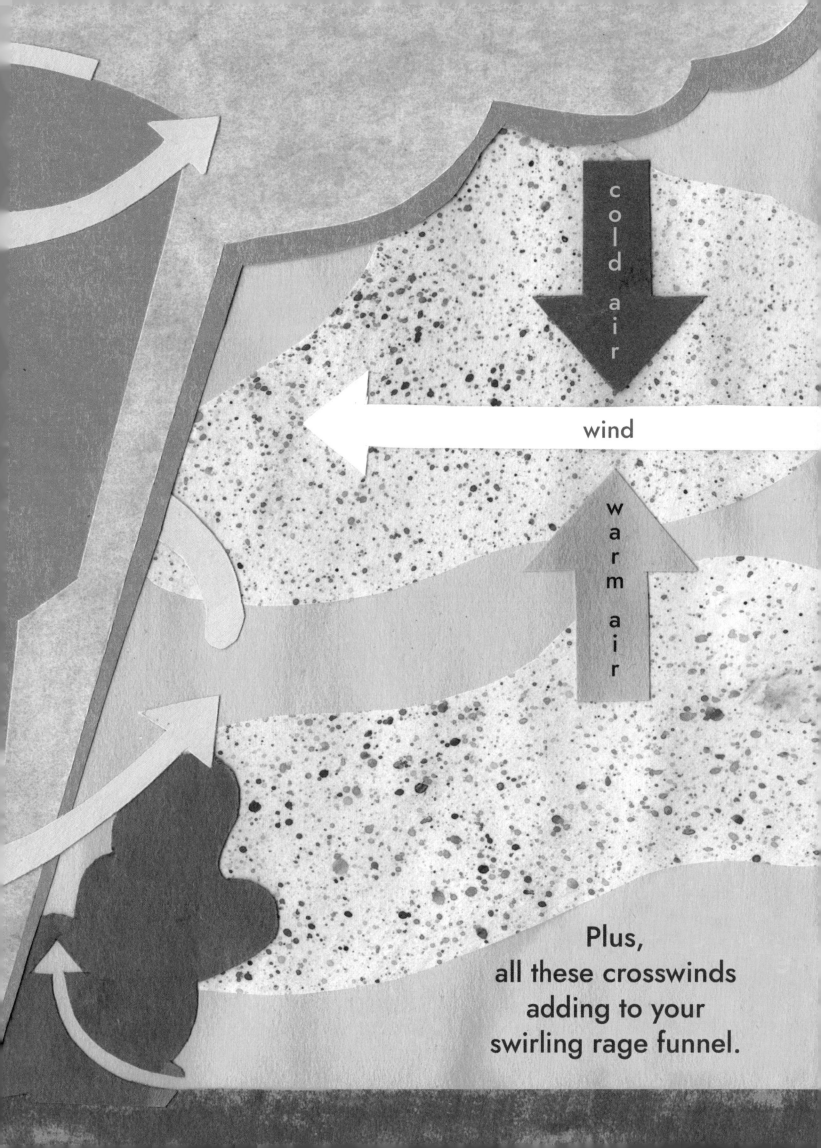

No wonder you would want to
spin so fast, yell so loud,
and throw so many things.

IT MAKES ME FEEL BETTER.

It must get exhausting, though.

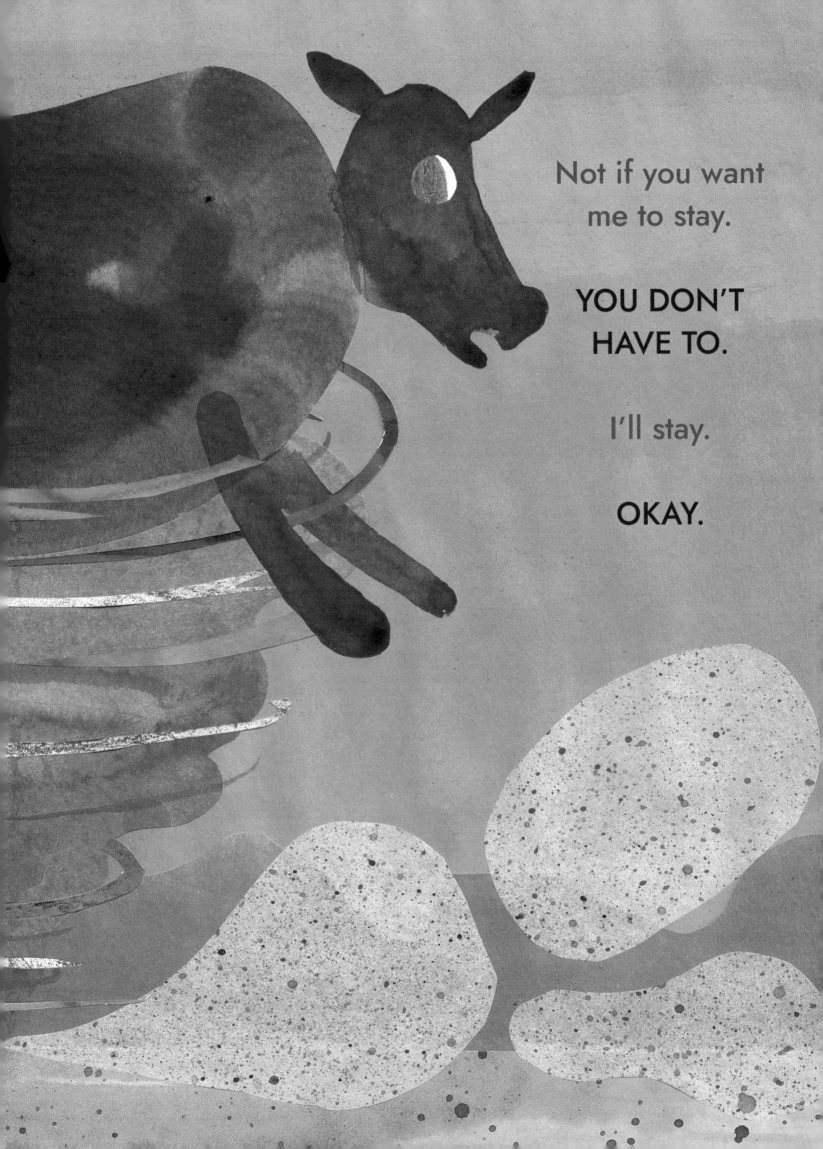

Not if you want
me to stay.

**YOU DON'T
HAVE TO.**

I'll stay.

OKAY.

COW,
MAYBE I'M NOT
SPINNING
AS RAPIDLY
AS I WAS
BEFORE.

That's alright.
You should rest.

BUT I'M NOT TIRED.

Maybe if we are quiet
and still for a minute . . .

REMEMBER
WHEN
I WAS SO BIG
AND
SO FAST?

Sshhhhhhhhhhhhh.

I'll be right here,
Tornado.